MONET
CHASES THE LIGHT

For Mum and Dad, Thanks, J.G.

Thank you to my son Ely, husband Wayne and my beautiful parents Ken and Elizabeth, for bringing much light into my world. Your love and support makes this all possible. - P.W.

Little Pink Dog Books,
PO Box 2039, Armidale, New South Wales 2350, Australia.
www.LittlePinkDogBooks.com

First published 2023

Production Management by Karen Small of smallbutmightyproductions.
Printed in China.

ISBN: 978-0-6454184-2-2 (hardback)

A catalogue record for this book is available from the National Library of Australia

MONET
CHASES THE LIGHT

Jenny Gahan & Patricia Ward

LITTLE PINK DOG BOOKS
Australia

Claude Monet was a French artist who loved to chase the light.

Each day he set out with his easel and box of bright colours to follow it wherever it went.

Monet chased the light as it frolicked through the
rolling fields and tickled the flowers.

He chased it as it danced through the treetops,
turning the leaves all shades of green.

He chased it as it skipped across the water, shimmering and sparkling.

The light teased Monet.
It never stayed still for long.

He painted quickly, using playful brushstrokes to catch
its slivers before they vanished, hidden by the clouds.

When the light was soft, Monet used gentle, flowing strokes.
When the light was strong, he used rough, choppy strokes.

Sometimes Monet used his boat as a floating studio.
He sailed up and down rivers chasing the light.

Monet liked to paint everyday things like the sunrise over the ocean, rocks on the beach or oats growing in the fields.

Sometimes Monet painted the same thing over and over, from dawn until dusk, watching the colours change as the sun moved across the sky.

He carried his canvases in a wheelbarrow, beginning a new painting
each time the light changed.

Monet moved into a pink house in a tiny French town called Giverny.

He planted gardens of flowers and made a beautiful
water lily pond.

Monet painted massive, magical pictures of his pond.

He painted at all times of the day, in sunshine, mist and rain.

His paintings glowed with colour, and still he chased the light, producing some of his most famous work.

As an old man, Monet grew tired of chasing the light.
He sat quietly beside his pond and watched as it
pranced through the lilies.

He watched the light
as it bounced across
the water making,
shadowy reflections.

Monet had spent his life chasing the light, catching it in his paintings.
But now, at last, the light had found him.